Be Polite

MY FIRST MANNERS

Written by Brent Cardillo and Elizabeth Clasing

Illustrated by Tom Brannon

This publication may not be reproduced in whole or in part by any means whatsoever without written permission from the copyright owners. Permission is never granted for commercial purposes.
Published by Louis Weber, C.E.O., Publications International, Ltd., 7373 North Cicero Avenue, Lincolnwood, Illinois 60712
Ground Floor, 59 Gloucester Place, London W1U 8JJ

Customer Service: 1-800-595-8484 or customer_service@pilbooks.com

www.pilbooks.com

p i kids is a registered trademark of Publications International, Ltd.

8 7 6 5 4 3 2 1

ISBN-13: 978-1-4127-6788-0   ISBN-10: 1-4127-6788-1

 publications international, ltd.

sesame workshop

Cookie, Cookie, cookie-eater,
Don't lick batter off the beater!

And if you start to chomp and chew,
Please keep your mouth closed
when you do!

Mount
Crunchmore

Humphrey Dumpty was at the hotel.
Humphrey Dumpty slipped and then fell.

Nobody giggled. He was helped to his feet.
To thank them, his helpers got cookies to eat.

Not-so-old Monster Hubbard

Went to her cupboard

To fetch her poor dog a bone.

She wanted to share,

But the cupboard was bare,

And so the poor dog had none.

But she didn't give up!

She went to the store.

Her pup was so happy

To find there was more.

And after sharing her dinner

Of bread and roast beef,

She was surprised and happy

To find him brushing his teeth!

Next day, Monster Hubbard

Looked in her cupboard,

And what do you think that she found?

Yes, nothing was there,

It was her dog's turn to share

A bone he had stashed in the ground.

Little Elmo met a fellow
Going to the fair.
Said Little Elmo to the fellow,
"Let me meet you there."
Said the fellow to Little Elmo,
"Here's what you should do.
Meet me at the Big-Top tent;
I'll see you there at two."

FAIR

And Little Elmo skipped away,

Then didn't know what to do.

Because Little Elmo couldn't tell time

To know when two was two.

He had an idea! He went to the fair

And asked a girl at the gate.

So Little Elmo did meet the fellow.

It's good manners not to be late!

Little Monster Blue,
Don't blow your horn!
The city is sleeping;
It's two in the morn.

Nighttime is for quiet;
Now it's noisy instead.
Please take your horn,
And go home to bed!